Franklin and the Stopwatch

From an episode of the animated TV series *Franklin*, produced by Nelvana Limited, Neurones France s.a.r.l. and Neurones Luxembourg S.A., based on the Franklin books by Paulette Bourgeois and Brenda Clark.

Story written by Sharon Jennings.
Illustrated by Sean Jeffrey, Sasha McIntyre and Jelena Sisic.
Based on the TV episode *Franklin's Stopwatch*, written by Brian Lasenby.

 Kids Can Read is a registered trademark of Kids Can Press Ltd.

Franklin

Kids Can Press acknowledges the financial support of the Government of Ontario, through the Ontario Media Development Corporation's Ontario Book Initiative; the Ontario Arts Council; the Canada Council for the Arts; and the Government of Canada, through the BPIDP, for our publishing activity.

Published in Canada by
Kids Can Press Ltd.
29 Birch Avenue
Toronto, ON M4V 1E2

Published in the U.S. by
Kids Can Press Ltd.
2250 Military Road
Tonawanda, NY 14150

www.kidscanpress.com

Series editor: Tara Walker
Edited by Yvette Ghione
Designed by Céleste Gagnon

Printed and bound in China

The hardcover edition of this book is smyth sewn casebound.
The paperback edition of this book is limp sewn with a drawn-on cover.

CM 07 0 9 8 7 6 5 4 3 2 1
CM PA 07 0 9 8 7 6 5 4 3 2 1

Library and Archives Canada Cataloguing in Publication

Jennings, Sharon
    Franklin and the stopwatch / written by Sharon Jennings ; illustrated by Sean Jeffrey, Sasha McIntyre, Jelena Sisic.

(Kids Can read)
The character Franklin was created by Paulette Bourgeois and Brenda Clark.

ISBN-13: 978-1-55337-890-7 (bound) ISBN-10: 1-55337-890-3 (bound)
ISBN-13: 978-1-55337-891-4 (pbk.) ISBN-10: 1-55337-891-1 (pbk.)

I. Jeffrey, Sean II. McIntyre, Sasha III. Sisic, Jelena IV. Bourgeois, Paulette V. Clark, Brenda VI Title. VII. Series: Kids Can read (Toronto, Ont.)

PS8569.E563F71745 2007   jC813'.54   C2005-907049-8

Kids Can Press is a **Corus™** Entertainment company

Franklin and the Stopwatch

Kids Can Press

Franklin can tie his shoes.

Franklin can count by twos.

And Franklin can do lots
of things that are lots of fun.

But not everyone thinks
all the things Franklin can do
are lots of fun.

This is a problem.

One day, Franklin looked

in the junk drawer.

"What's this?" he asked.

"That's a stopwatch," said his father.

Franklin put it
to his ear.

"It sure is,"
said Franklin.
"This watch
has stopped."

Franklin's father held up the stopwatch.

"When I say 'go,' hold your breath,"

he said.

His father pushed a button

and said "Go!"

Franklin held

his breath.

Soon, Franklin stopped

holding his breath.

His father pushed the button again.

"You held your breath

for ten seconds," he said.

"I get it!" said Franklin.

"A stopwatch doesn't *tell* time.

It *times* time."

Franklin wanted to play

with the stopwatch.

He timed his mother on the phone.

"Ten minutes!"

said Franklin.

"You sure talk a lot."

His mother frowned.

"Why don't you go outside?" she said.

Franklin went outside.

He timed his father weeding the garden.

"It's been fifteen minutes!" said Franklin.

"You haven't done very much."

His father frowned.

"Why don't you go to the park?" he said.

Franklin went to the park.

Beaver and Bear were playing.

Franklin showed them his stopwatch.

He showed them how it worked.

"Do something," said Franklin.

"I'll time you."

Beaver slid down the slide.

"Eight seconds!" said Franklin.

Bear swung on a swing.

"Twenty-five seconds!"

said Franklin.

Beaver hung from the monkey bars.

"Thirty seconds!" said Franklin.

Bear ran around the soccer field.

"Two minutes!" said Franklin.

"Do something else."

"No," said Bear. "I'm tired."

Everyone went to the pond.

"It took us four minutes and two seconds

to get here," said Franklin.

"Forget about the stopwatch," said Beaver.

"Let's play."

Beaver swam across the pond.

"Eighteen seconds!"

said Franklin.

Bear rowed under the bridge.

"Thirty-five seconds!" said Franklin.

"Stop the stopwatch!" said Bear.

"Just play!"

"I'm hungry," said Beaver.

"Let's go for ice cream."

Everyone went

to the ice cream shop.

"It took us three minutes

to get here,"

said Franklin.

Beaver and Bear bought ice cream cones.

"Don't you want a cone?" asked Bear.

"No," said Franklin. "I'll time you eating."

He started the stopwatch.

Beaver and Bear ate their ice cream cones.

"Four minutes!" said Franklin.

"You are driving me crazy!" said Beaver.

"I'm going to the library."

"Me too," said Bear.

Franklin started the stopwatch.

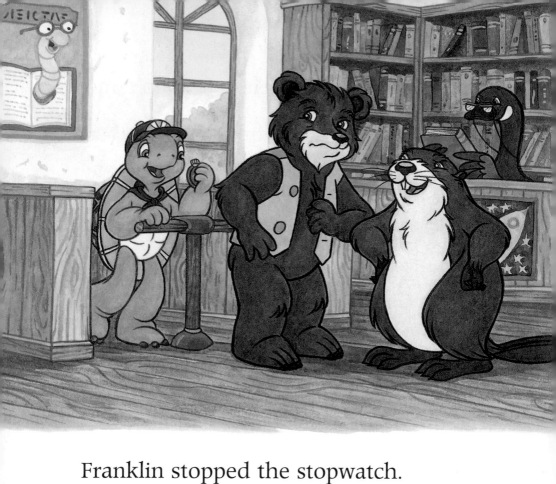

Franklin stopped the stopwatch.

"It took us four minutes

and fifteen seconds to get to the library,"

he said. "Now I'll time you

choosing a book."

"I have a better idea," said Beaver.

She reached over and took the stopwatch.

"We'll time *you!*"

"But it's *my* stopwatch," said Franklin.

Beaver started the stopwatch.

"Hurry up, Franklin,"

she said.

"Choose a book."

Franklin chose *Dynaroo Saves the Day.*

"Twenty-five seconds!"

said Beaver.

"Can I have my

stopwatch back?"

said Franklin.

"Nope," said Bear.

"Start reading."

He started

the stopwatch.

"I'm going to the park
to read," said Franklin.

"Okay," said Bear.

"We'll time you walking."

Franklin frowned.

Then he hurried out of the library.

Franklin got as far as the ice cream shop.

"Stop the stopwatch," he said.

"I want an ice cream cone."

Franklin ordered his cone.

"Okay," said Beaver.

"We'll time you eating."

"I'll eat at the park,"

said Franklin.

"Then let's go!" said Bear.

He started the stopwatch again.

Franklin frowned.

Then he hurried

to the park.

Bear stopped the stopwatch.

"It took us two minutes

to get here,"

he said.

"Forget about

the stopwatch!"

yelled Franklin.

"Nope," said Bear.

"This stopwatch is fun!"

Franklin frowned.

He licked his ice cream cone.

"Mmmm," said Franklin.

"I love fly-fly-berry-berry!"

Then he opened his book.

"I love Dynaroo!"

said Franklin.

"Hurry up, Franklin," said Bear.

"I have to go home soon."

Franklin licked his ice cream carefully.

He turned a page slowly.

"You're taking a long time," said Beaver.

"I sure am," agreed Franklin.

Then he reached for the stopwatch.

He pushed in the button.

"What are you doing?" asked Beaver.

Franklin smiled.

"Sometimes a stopwatch

needs to stop watching!"